# The Christmas Painting

## Enchanted Holidays Series – Book 1

# AVERY GALE

Cover Design by Jess Buffett
Editing by Sandy Ebel

Published by Avery Gale

Thank you for respecting the hard work of this author.

This is a work of fiction. Names, places, characters and incidents either are the product of the author's imagination or are used fictitiously and any resemblance to any actual persons, living or dead, organizations, events or locales are entirely coincidental.

If you find any books being sold or shared illegally, please contact the author at avery.gale@ymail.com.

# Prologue

"HOW OLD ARE you, Freddie?"

"Thirty-two."

"Wow, you're almost as old as my mama."

Freddie grinned as he brushed the snow from his favorite seat beside the steps of the gazebo. "Someday, thirty-two won't seem so old to you, my sweet Adilei." The tiny snowballs he threw at her burst into sparkling droplets of water when they touched Adi's skin. "I've been thirty-two forever, Adilei."

"Forever? Why?"

"It's how the magic works. I'm waiting for my one."

"Your one?"

"The one whose smile lights up the world around her. The one who can see me when others can't. The one who loves me above all others. She'll be able to free me from the painting, Princess."

"I wish I could pull you right out of that painting today, Freddie. You're my best friend."

"Princess, you're the light of my life, but you can't free me from the painting, today. It's not our time."

"I don't understand."

"You will, Princess. Someday, you will."

1

# Chapter One

A DILEI KENT STARED blankly at her family's enormous Boston mansion. She hadn't been *home* in nearly a decade, but it seemed like only yesterday she'd been unceremoniously escorted to the waiting car by her father's unyielding butler. Marcus Lloyd had been her father's loyal right hand for as long as Adi could remember. He'd always served as a sentinel between her father and the outside world, and Adi had definitely been an outsider after her mother died.

It hadn't been a surprise to hear her father and Marcus had passed within days of each other. The condolence card she'd sent to Marcus' family had been returned unopened, and she hadn't taken time to find out if there were other relatives. She'd simply torn up the memorial check and the card before tossing the pieces into the fireplace of her small beach bungalow.

Taking a deep breath, she climbed the steps to the front door. Adi tried to push aside the feeling of unease sweeping over her, chalking it up to exhaustion; traveling always drained her. A cool breeze brushed over her cheek in a silent caress. She shuddered beneath her wool coat, but she wasn't sure if it was because she was chilled or from the odd sense of intimacy the wisp of air left behind.

"See? This is why I should have stayed in Miami. It's warm. And the white covering the ground is soft, warm sand rather than snow up to my ass…ets. And the lulling sound of the surf beating against the shore is comforting, unlike the howling wind screeching an unnecessary warning about the coming blizzard. I should have my head checked for not waiting until spring to deal with this."

By the time the elderly driver finished lugging her bulky bags up the stairs and into the foyer, he was panting. He nodded gratefully at the generous tip she handed him before disappearing back into his sleek black Towne Car. Looking up and down the street, Adi wondered if she would know any of her neighbors. Would any of the faces be familiar and or would they all be strangers? *I guess it doesn't really matter since I won't be home long to find out.*

The irony of being *home* wasn't lost on her. Her position at the resort had been cut the same day her father's attorney called to say she needed to return to Boston to finalize the sale of the Commonwealth Avenue mansion her family had called home for generations. She'd always loved the five-story, red brick building, complete with its turrets and dormers. The curving walnut banister in the front foyer had been too tempting, and she'd slid down it so many times, the caretaker had been forced to re-varnish it at least once a year. She'd missed it when her father insisted she attend boarding school after her mother's death. It wasn't until she was much older she understood he'd been trying to protect her from his own overwhelming grief.

Stepping into the front hall, Adi was surprised to find the empty house toasty warm and smelling of freshly baked bread. Something tickled in the back of her mind, but before she could pull it to the forefront, the jangling of the phone she'd slipped into her coat pocket distracted her. Her father's long-time attorney's, Malcolm Bradley, clipped greeting made Adi roll her eyes. She'd never met anyone more uptight than the man who'd looked two days older than dirt when she was in elementary school. *Cripes, I'll bet he whistles like a damned teapot when he farts.*

"Ms. Kent. The caretaker wasn't available to turn on the heat in your father's… well, I suppose it's *your* house now. Anyway, I'd suggest you stay at a local hotel until later in the week. The house has been closed for some time, so it will need aired out, and it will take me a few days to find someone to freshen things up."

*Say what?*

"I'm not sure what you mean, Mr. Bradley. I'm standing in the house now. It's warm and smells as if someone has been baking." There was nothing but silence on the other end for so long she was beginning to think they'd been disconnected. "Are you still there?"

"That's not possible. I'm sure you must be mistaken."

*Mistaken? I'm standing in the damned house, you pompous ass.*

"You and the caretaker have the only two keys. He called me just a few moments ago to tell me he's in the hospital and has been there for the past several days. I'd hoped to catch you before you found a taxi."

On the one hand, it was vaguely amusing to hear the puckered-ass attorney sounding off-center. But it was also unsettling to know someone had, not only been able to enter the house, but it seemed plausible they'd known when she was arriving.

"I'm going to look around and see if I can figure out who I have to thank for making sure I had a warm place to sleep. I'll be in touch." She heard the man suck in a breath, but didn't wait for his response before disconnecting the call.

Adi wasn't entirely sure why she'd let Malcom Bradley annoy her, but had the strangest feeling he knew or at least suspected, who'd been responsible for her warm welcome. Suspecting he knew and wasn't telling her didn't set well. If he didn't want her to stay at the house, why had he given the key to the driver he'd sent to meet her? *Wait, did he say taxi?* The elderly man must be slipping if he'd forgotten he'd sent a driver to meet her.

Shrugging off the questions rolling through her mind, Adi wandered through the expansive first floor. Everything was exactly as it had been ten years ago, and she suspected nothing had been changed since long before she'd been born. Adi couldn't remember a single element of the décor ever looking any different than it did right at this moment. *How odd.*

"I wonder if the Christmas painting is still here?" She and her father had argued about the large oil painting in her suite of rooms the day she'd left. Adi had wanted to take it with her when she'd moved to college, but her father had been adamant it not leave the house. They'd disagreed, and she'd finally resigned herself to leaving it behind. And then they'd argued about it again when she moved to Florida; that disagreement had escalated so quickly, she'd wondered many times over the years how they'd allowed a painting to come between them.

Her father's insistence the four-by-three-foot depiction of Christmastime in Victorian Era Boston remain in her suite of rooms had never bothered her until then. She'd always loved the painting…there was something almost magical about it. As a child, she'd believed the people in the large work of art could talk to her. Before her mother died, Adi would lay at her side and describe the conversations she had with the people braving the falling snow to walk the picturesque streets of Boston during the holidays.

Even as a six-year-old, Adi understood people in paintings weren't supposed to talk. As an adult looking back, she realized as her mother's conditioned worsened, the characters in the painting interacted more often. During her first year at the university, Adi had finally confided in a counselor who assured her the mind had an amazing ability to invent ways to cope with stress. "I'm not surprised you found comfort in the figures in a painting you loved. What I do find odd is you're still focused on it so many years later." The stern woman's censure had stung, and Adi had never mentioned the painting to anyone again.

Pulling herself out of the melancholy of those memories, Adi wandered into the formal living room. Stepping in front of the stone fireplace, her eyes filled with tears as she looked up at the portrait hanging above the mantle. Soft brown eyes, so like her own, smiled down at her, the gentle curve of her mother's lips tilting up. Her father had commissioned the painting as soon as he learned her mother was ill. Adi hadn't understood how devastating losing his wife had been for her dad until years later. Regret squeezed her chest as she thought about all the opportunities she'd missed to repair her relationship with her father.

"Don't go there, girl. Regrets won't change anything." *Dandy, now I'm talking to myself.*

ADI ROLLED HER luggage into the small elevator, but decided to eat before heading up to her fourth-floor suite. Laughing at herself when she realized she'd closed the decorative metal, folding gate of the elevator, she shook her head and turned down the hall. Her dad had always been completely anal about keeping the gate closed. Adi had never understood his obsession, it had just been easier to pull the creaking metal shut than to listen to him lecture her if she left it open.

A half hour later, she'd polished off the roast beef dinner she found in the refrigerator and uncorked the cheapest bottle of wine she could find in the small wine fridge. Looking around the kitchen, Adi had to admit the designer had done an amazing job with the recent remodel. The bathrooms and kitchen were the only rooms in the house which had been updated. Every other room in the house had been restored to its original glory during what had to be the most costly and extensive private restoration on Commonwealth in history.

Just because she hadn't been home, didn't mean she hadn't been consulted about the restoration. Her father had insisted she be involved and at several points during the two-year project, she'd wanted to pull her hair out when his questions about minutia had come almost hourly. But the finished product was stunning. Once again, the weight of her guilt made it feel like someone was squeezing her heart. The last argument she'd had with her dad should never have happened, and even though they'd talked often after that day, things had never been the same. Damnit, she'd known he'd never let her take the painting. And even though she'd wanted it in the small bungalow she'd rented, it was far too valuable to move from place to place. *Freddie told me... the magic only works in this house.*

"Well, no more wine for me. When I start quoting my imaginary friend, it's time to go to bed. And God bless it, I'm talking to myself again." Moving to the elevator, she slid the gate open and stared into the empty space.

# Chapter Two

FREDDIE WATCHED FROM the shadows as Adilei stared into the empty elevator. Even if the dark circles under her eyes hadn't told him she was exhausted, the fact she hadn't heard the elevator moving *twice* would have given it away.

"I've been waiting for you, my love. Yes, indeed, waiting so very long. Welcome home." He'd barely whispered the words, but he saw her shudder and look side to side. She seemed to sense she wasn't alone, but she'd had enough wine to dull any fear the feeling might have elicited. He'd looked on as she searched the small wine fridge for the least expensive bottle, but since he'd personally stocked the racks with ten of her dad's best, her effort had been an exercise in futility. "You've always been frugal, sweetheart, but I'm going to teach you there is no shame in enjoying wealth as long as you aren't being wasteful. Spreading your good fortune should never make you feel guilty." There were very few people who understood the importance of balancing living well and being responsible.

Freddie had become trapped in the painting when he'd foolishly made a deal with one of hell's minions. Trusting the wrong man had nearly cost his family everything. The price for using his magic for monetary gain? Confinement in the Kent household until his soulmate set him free. The first several decades he'd spent trapped in the Christmas scene without the ability to communicate with the outside world. The painting was an exact replica of the city he'd once considered his for the taking. Freddie had been forced to stand for years in the exact spot where he'd been when he'd pleaded for mercy. The head of the wizard council had outlined the terms, then vanished into the frigid winter air. That moment in time had been frozen forever, immortalized in oils before magically appearing in the top floor suite of the Kent mansion.

The moment he recognized Adilei as the other half of his soul was still as vivid in his memory as the day it happened. She'd only been a few months old when her nanny sat her in an intricately carved highchair facing the Christmas painting. He'd waved at her and joked with one of the men standing nearby that the baby knew they were real. Her violet eyes had widened, and she'd squealed, clapping her small, chubby hands with obvious delight.

The realization she had indeed seen them shocked him to the tips of his toes. He'd been unable to move for several seconds, his eyes locked with hers as she tilted her head to the side and watched him. It was a gesture he'd see repeated many times as she grew into the stunning woman standing before him. Anytime she was trying to solve a puzzle, she'd tilt her head as if the altered view would make the solution easier to see. Their souls had been fused in that brief moment of eye contact, everything changed between one heartbeat and the next.

As if she'd heard his musings, Adilei tilted her head to the side as she stared into the empty elevator car. Even now, twenty-eight years later, the gesture still made him smile. Freddie pushed a comforting thought into Adilei's mind, assuring her the bags were safely in her suite. Her soul had always been open to his, and today was no different.

The magic inside her was strong, but unrealized. *How could any woman have so much and be so unaware?* Shrugging her shoulders, she pulled the gate closed and turned to the stairs. That was his sweet Princess; she'd never liked the small elevator, shuddering when she'd told her father it felt like a cage.

Emmett Kent III had never understood his tempestuous daughter and spent very little time trying. Her internal conflict stemmed from knowing she was different, but not understanding why, and Emmett hadn't taken the time to unravel the mystery which swirled within his only child.

The elder Kent had been as obsessed with success as his great-great-grandfather had been, but Adilei's father lacked the compassion his namesake had shown those in his inner circle. If not for his friend's generosity, Frederick's folly would have devastated the Johnson financial legacy. Emmett Kent had stepped in when Freddie's other friends had turned their backs on him. He'd been warned against using magic to make money, but had been too arrogant to even consider the rules might actually apply to him.

The Kent family had been sheltering him for more than a century. Now it was time to rejoin the world he'd been forced to observe from the confines of a picture frame. Those first decades, when he'd only been able to hear everyone around him without answering, had been torturous. For the next several decades, he'd only been able to communicate with the other figures in the paining.

Adilei's mother, Lizette, had been the first one outside the painting who could hear him. As her health failed, their conversations became more heartfelt. He'd marveled at the magic in her and was forever grateful for her friendship. It had been her spell which allowed them to move from one painting to another and to inhabit the house for brief periods of time.

Lizette had been more than ready to return to the other side; the pain had been unbearable, but the treatments had been worse. The night she died, she made him promise he'd watch over Adilei. Lizette's only regret was leaving her young daughter with a father who'd never understood her.

Losing his wife had cost Emmett Kent a piece of his soul he had never been able to recover. Freddie's debt to the financial wizards of Wall Street had long since been paid and his fortune restored. The only thing left to do was claim the woman who could break the final tethers of the spell. The only problem? She'd never believe in her own magic. Freddie worried the only way to show her how truly special she was would be to take her into the painting. *Getting in would be easy. Getting back out, much more difficult.*

ADI STUMBLED DOWN four flights of stairs the next morning after a restless night spent tossing and turning, looking almost worse than when she'd gone to bed. Freddie had shaken his head as he'd watched her roll around, alone, in the large bed, wondering how much better she'd sleep after a few Earth shattering orgasms.

He'd been mesmerized watching her don a pair of skin tight jeans and overly large sweatshirt before making her way downstairs this morning. It really was a pity to cover up such physical perfection, but he'd be the first to admit, women's undergarments had improved enormously since he'd personally last seen them. Over the years, he'd seen many packages delivered from Victoria's Secret, but today was the first time he hadn't turned away when Adilei was dressing. *For what it's worth, I think Victoria should stop keeping such tempting treasures secret.*

The original owners of the house would laugh themselves silly if they had lived to see him turning away when his beautiful Princess changed her clothes. They would have no doubt been amazed to learn how times had changed inside the walls of what had once been one of the most prominent brothels in Boston.

Emmett Kent had run a number of successful businesses, but none had been more profitable than the Templar's Rose. The obvious reference to the Knights Templar comparison of a woman's sex to the petals of a blooming rose was lost on many of the city's prudish population. But it was an open invitation to anyone who understood the true meaning of inscription above the door. *In rosaria Paesti.* Roses did indeed bloom within.

Freddie laughed to himself when Adilei shivered, walking down the sweeping staircase leading to the expansive foyer. Even though the house was warm, her blood had probably thinned considerably during her years in Florida. It would to take her a while to reacclimate to the colder climes of the northeast. He only hoped he could convince her to stay. Knowing the weasel Emmett had employed as an attorney, he would be doing his best to convince her to sell the home that had been in her family for almost two centuries.

Shaking his head, Freddie refused to give those thoughts any more of his attention. The ramifications would be far reaching and devastating to more people than he wanted to think about—himself included. He set his jaw and steeled his resolve. Failure was not an option. Too many people were depending on him. His entire future was in the soft hands currently pouring the coffee he'd made for her into one of the delicate china cups which had served generations of Kents.

"I don't know who made coffee, but I'm going to marry them," Adilei's voice was reverent as she sipped the special blend her father always ordered.

"Good to know." Hearing his deep voice right behind her made Adi jump and let loose a blood-curdling scream. She spun so quickly, she lost her balance. If Freddie hadn't reached out to steady her, she'd have gone down in a tangle of arms and legs at his feet. He set her cup back on the counter, but continued to hold her arm. He could sense her first instinct was to flee, but the instant his hands wrapped around her upper arms, Freddie was able to infuse her with a sense of calm. "Easy, Princess."

"Freddie? How? How did you… it's not possible?" Confusion clouded her violet eyes, but he was relieved she didn't appear to be frightened.

"Come on. I'll get my coffee and we'll talk. I have a lot to tell you." He poured his own coffee and followed her. Sitting at the small bistro table near the French doors, he sipped his coffee and looked out over the courtyard with longing. He could hardly wait for the day he could once again step outside the confines of the house. Taking a sip, he smiled as it warmed him from the inside out. For years he'd been tortured by the smell of coffee brewing, unable to get any for himself. But during the last few years, he'd enjoyed sharing coffee with the other figures from the painting while they'd renovated the large house.

It amused him how some of the original cast from the Commonwealth Street Christmas scene had branched out to other paintings. Some had grown tired of the perpetual winter and moved to the more moderate climes of tropical scenes. Craftsmen wanted to be able to build again, so they'd moved to a depiction of post-World War II New York until they'd been released to work around the house. The farmers and ranchers had happily migrated to the Kent Family's collection of Frederic Remington paintings in library. The ladies who'd settled in a Parisian scene in the living room were responsible for the dinner Adilei had eaten last night.

They enjoyed the silence for several minutes before he picked up their cups and returned to the kitchen to refill them. She watched him from the table and arched a brow when he poured cream into her cup and added the right amount of sugar.

"Princess, I've been watching you prepare your coffee since before you were old enough to drink it. I know what you like." When she started to speak, he shook his head. "Of course, it's real cream. Your ancestors would haunt me until my dying day if I served you anything else. And that's not taking into account the ire I'd face from the good ladies from the living room painting."

"You mean there are others? Are there really more people living in the... well, living here?"

# Chapter Three

ADI FELT LIKE she'd fallen through Alice's looking glass, her entire world felt like it was tilting precariously on its axis. Another few seconds of this conversation and the Earth might well tumble off into space, never to be heard from again.

"Adilei, take a breath, sweetheart. You are turning a very interesting shade of blue." Freddie's voice brought her back to the moment. She sucked in a deep breath, relieved when the black dots clouding her vision evaporated.

"It's all just so incredibly surreal. Discovering our conversations weren't just my imagination is a huge relief." She didn't try to hold back her snicker. "A college counselor insisted it was the only way my young mind could cope with the grief when my mother died. I'd sure love to rub this in her face… but something tells me that won't be an option."

Freddie rolled his eyes before focusing his intense gaze on her. "Those who don't possess magic can't see it. If they can't see it, they don't believe it exists. In other words, if they can't see what you see, then there must be something wrong with YOU."

Their conversation meandered through their shared

memories, and Adi found herself laughing at some of the sweet moments she'd forgotten. It had been easy to forget how many happy memories she'd made here; a new wave of regret washed over her. How different would things have been if she had swallowed her pride and admitted she was wrong? By the time they got around to discussing the history of the house, they'd started on their second pot of coffee.

Shaking her head, Adi chuckled, "A house of ill repute? Seriously?" Her great-great something or other had made at least part of the family fortune running a cat house?

OVER THE PAST two days, she'd listened to Freddie and his friends describe how each of them had ended up trapped in the painting. Each story was slightly different, but there was one recurring theme... they'd used their magic in a way which was against some ancient code. It was a lot to take in, but she found herself riveted by their tales. Many had been trapped for years, but Freddie was the only one who'd been confined for multiple generations.

"Tell me how the house has changed since it served the vices of Boston's elite." Adi was finally able to think about how her home had once been used without blushing, but she was still struggling with the fact Freddie had been a frequent visitor. For the first time in her life, Adi felt a pang of jealousy she wasn't quite sure how to handle.

During their long conversations, Freddie had rarely left her side. His touch was becoming more and more intimate, and she was beginning to crave it more each day. He hadn't made any overt moves to seduce her, and as strange as it seemed, Adi was starting to wonder if she'd misread the increasingly personal contact between them.

"Aside from technology, it's changed very little. Some of the furnishings are original, but most of the original upholstered items have been replaced with period appropriate pieces. I've always admired your family's adherence to the spirit of their contract with the wizard council."

*Contract?* Freddie must have noted my confusion because his smile became wistful, and he nodded.

He briefly explained the inner workings of the governing body of the world's witches and warlocks. But it was their promise to protect the members of the Kent family as long as the house remained in the possession of a Kent which fascinated her. She was surprised by his willingness to share so much information about a group she assumed valued a certain level of anonymity and told him so.

"They are only secret because no one believes magic is real, Princess. The non-magical world is very skeptical. Quite frankly, I'm astonished religion is as universally accepted as it is. People have become more open-minded in so many ways, but their hearts have become less open to the mysteries of the unknown." Freddie told her, in his opinion, scientists had done humankind a great disservice by teaching them everything *real* required proof.

"Why? Because people are generally of the *I have to see it to believe it* mindset?" She agreed with his observation, but was interested in his reasoning. She'd always enjoyed talking to Freddie; he was not only intelligent, he was observant and insightful.

"No. Because they can see it and still not believe it. Most people refuse to believe anything they can't explain." She'd never considered the difference, but knew the truth when she heard it. Everyone else had drifted back to their respective paintings, leaving Adi and Freddie lounging on the large sofa in the den, watching the final credits of an old movie scroll up the screen. When she started to stir, he pulled her back against his side.

"Stay, Princess. I enjoy having you snuggled up against me. I've waited a very long time to have you in my arms."

Adi settled back and tried to take a deep breath. She could almost hear the sizzling sexual energy moving between them.

"Did you have girlfriends in the paintings?" The minute the words left her mouth, Adi dropped her face into her hands. Her cheeks were instantly red hot, and she knew her blush had probably painted her crimson, head to toe. "Oh God, I'm sorry. That was completely out of line. It's really none of my business."

"Look at me, Adilei." He waited until she'd dropped her hands and turned her face to him before continuing, "I'm not going to deny I was a rogue in my younger days. Not being able to indulge in pleasures of the flesh was a part of my punishment for the first several decades. Then there was you."

She felt her eyes widen in surprise at his comment.

"It's true, Princess. Once I recognized you as the one I had been waiting for, it was easy to set those desires aside. I would have never risked what I wanted to build with you by making a stitch."

"Excuse me?" How had they switched from sex to sewing?

"When I was younger, making a stitch meant having a casual sexual relationship." He grinned and pressed a quick kiss to her forehead. "I've listened to language evolve, but sometimes it's easier to revert back to what I knew."

"DON'T LET OTHERS define your reality." The memory came back to Adi in rush. Freddie had told her that many times over the years, but she hadn't understood the full meaning of his words until now. Groaning, she shook her head at her own naivete, remembering it was one of the last things he'd said to her before she moved to Florida.

God, she'd wanted to take the painting with her. She'd been so terribly lonely those first months, she'd almost moved home. It didn't matter that she'd been forced to attend boarding schools after her mother died, or that she'd also spent her college years away from home. "You told me that."

"Many times. It was one of the things I promised Lizette." Adilei's eyes widened at the mention of her mother.

"You talked to my mother?" The reverence in her voice had been tinged with envy she couldn't hold back.

"And everyone else in your family, Princess."

"But you said only those who are magical can…" she let the words fade away when the corners of his mouth tilted up. Smile lines at the corners of his eyes did nothing to detract from his handsome face. He hadn't aged in all the years she'd known him. Something about that tickled the back of her mind, but the touch of his fingers trailing down the side of her face pulled her attention back to their conversation.

"Everyone in the paintings is paying some kind of debt to a witch or wizard though no one has been here as long as I have. Most are forced into a life of service for a few decades, not generations."

Adi couldn't imagine the heartbreak those locked in the paintings must have felt knowing the world would be an entirely different place when they were finally freed. "Everyone they care about is gone or they've grown so old there's nothing left of the relationship." The cruelty was almost impossible to comprehend, but in many ways, she'd condemned herself to a life remarkably similar to the one forced on others isolating herself in Florida. "Do your families know where you are? Do they ever come to visit?" Adi searched her memory, but couldn't remember anyone visiting the paintings. "I don't think that's something I'd forget."

"Yes, they know. At least those who care enough to make the effort can easily find out where we are. Most are too frightened of the magic to come here, and in truth, it's pointless because we can't talk to them. It's part of the debt." Freddie's eyes were filled with regret, and she wondered how much guilt he was still carrying for the heartbreak he'd brought his family.

"How many paintings in the house are…"

"Enchanted?" For the first time since they'd started this conversation, his smile seemed to reach his eyes. She was relieved to see a glimmer of the fun-loving Freddie she'd always sworn was her best friend, no matter how great the difference in their ages. "The Christmas Painting in your suite is the only one where we could live when we're first send here. Eventually, we were able to move between the paintings to better serve our hosts."

Her head was beginning to throb; it was too much to absorb. Pinching the bridge of her nose, Adi willed the caffeine from her soda to kick in and push back the fatigue threatening to pull her under. She didn't realize she'd closed her eyes until strong hands began massaging the tight muscles along the tops of her shoulders. In many ways, it felt odd knowing Freddie was touching her, but at the same time, it felt like the most natural thing in the world. His strong hands melted the tension pulling her muscles tight as bowstrings. When she moaned softly, Freddie's hands stilled for just a moment before she felt his warm breath waft over the sensitive skin on the side of her neck.

"I've waited a very long time to hear that sweet sound, Princess. I'm looking forward to learning all the sexy sounds you make when I touch you. I'll explore every inch of you and map each of your sensitive spots." She shuddered as the heat of desire flooded every cell of her body. "Soon, my sweet Adilei. Very soon."

# Chapter Four

A DILEI SAT BEHIND her father's enormous mahogany desk, listening to Malcom Bradley drone on about the minutia of her father's will. She hoped she didn't look as stupid as he believed her to be. The man was doing a very poor job of concealing his insistence she sell the house. What she had yet to figure out was why he was so adamant.

"Are you questioning his motives, yet, Adilei?" Freddie's question, spoken from his position behind the elderly lawyer, made her smile.

"I'm not sure what you find so amusing about your responsibilities, Ms. Kent, but I assure you the sale of this house is going to be a very complicated endeavor. You're lucky I promised your father I'd handle all the dreary details for you."

*Oh yeah, lucky me.* The man couldn't care less about her best interests.

"He's trying to sell you a dog, Princess." She wasn't sure what Freddie meant, and he must have sensed her question. "He's lying. He's going to line his pockets with this sale, but I think there is more."

She agreed. In Adi's opinion, it was obvious he was working for someone. It was equally obvious that someone was not her. The first time Mr. Bradley had come to the house, she'd watched in stunned wonder as Freddie and several other people from the painting wandered through the room without Malcolm batting an eye. The old man was completely oblivious there were several others in the room, and he'd used the perceived privacy to blow enough smoke up her ass to make her worry she might float to the ceiling.

Adi had to admit, the numbers he floated as reasonable sale prices far exceeded her wildest estimate. She'd be able to buy her own Caribbean island with that much money. She'd been intent on selling the enormous mansion when she returned home, but now, she wasn't sure that's what she wanted to do. The more she learned about the history of her ancestral home, the more difficult it was to see herself parting with it. As Malcolm Bradley droned on, she made note of several questions she wanted answers to before making a final decision.

"Don't forget to read those contracts, Ms. Kent. The real estate agents want to list the property immediately. I'd suggest you get some Christmas decorations up right away. Potential buyers will want to see what the place looks like decorated. Women are always envisioning where they'll put a tree when they look at a house."

His last comment struck her as odd for a couple of reasons. First, how did he know that unless he was closely associated with a real estate business. And if he was a part of an agency which one on the short list he'd given her was his? And second, his assumption that women base their real estate decisions on the ideal place to showcase their Christmas tree was positively insulting. By the time he shuffled out the front door into the biting winter wind, she was ready to pull her hair out.

"I think if you'll do a bit of research, you'll find all the real estate agencies listed are shadows of the first one on the list. His son is listed as the owner, but that's in name only. The younger man is a puppet. His dad pulls the strings."

Turning to Freddie, she raised her brow in question. "How do you know this? You've been stuck inside this house for more than a century."

"I sat in on his meetings with your father and grandfather. Your dad held him in check for the most part, but your grandfather played looser with the rules. I wouldn't say your granddad was shady, but he was inclined to believe the rules didn't apply to him." Adi could tell Freddie had tempered his words. When she didn't respond, he continued, "As much as I hate to admit it, I was worse. I used my magic when I shouldn't have. Thank God, Emmett was smart enough to walk away from the demon I'd aligned myself with, or he wouldn't have been able to offer a solution."

They'd touched on this briefly in their previous conversations, but she still could barely imagine the grief of losing the ability to communicate with your family and friends. Being forced to stand silently by and watch the world around you would be a special kind of torment. Deciding it was time to divert the conversation, she asked, "Tell me more about the painting. How did it come to be enchanted? Was it painted with people in it?"

Much to her relief, he laughed out loud. "So many

questions, Princess." Pulling her to her feet, he took her hand in his and turned to the stairs. "Come on. Let's go upstairs. I want to show you something I think you may have forgotten."

A few minutes later, they were standing, hand in hand, in front of the painting, and Adi felt some of her favorite childhood memories come flooding back. The colors were as vivid as they were the first time she remembered looking at the winter scene. The Christmas tree lights almost sparkled, and the snow glistened under the gas street lamps. Boughs of holly were draped around the half walls of the gazebo, and lights twinkled around the top. The street vendors were selling hot chocolate and cider while others peddled baked treats. People were wrapped in their winter woolens, their cheeks rosy from the cold; most were smiling as the Christmas spirit seems to have settled over the decorated divide of Commonwealth Avenue.

"Was it really this beautiful?" She'd always assumed it was too picturesque to have been real.

"Yes, it was. The artist painted it for a very special young lady, his daughter, who loved the Christmas season. She'd spend hours wandering through scenes, just like this one, enjoying the ambiance. The young girl was beloved by everyone who knew her. When she was thrown from her horse and paralyzed, the entire city grieved."

"Her father painted the picture?"

"Yes, he was a talented artist, but not well known." Adi watched a group of boys run from one end of the painting to the other, throwing snowballs at each other, laughing when their icy missiles hit their target. "It turns out, the young girl had unknowingly befriended an ancient wizard. He'd been sitting on one of the park benches, disguised in an old tattered coat. She brought him a cup of hot soup, assuming he was down on his luck. When the wizard heard about the girl's accident, he stopped by to visit her. Of course, he was dressed to the nines, so she didn't recognize him. To his dismay, she treated him with the same courtesy both times.

"On the way out of the house, he spoke with her father who was worried about how his daughter would cope with being housebound during the upcoming holidays. Knowing she would never be able to ice skate in the park or enjoy any of the winter fun she loved was weighing heavily on his mind. He showed the visitor the painting he was working on, and the wizard was so touched by his kindness, he revealed himself to the father. It turns out his daughter had given a cup of broth to the head of the Wizards Council."

"Did the girl's father believe him?" She couldn't hold the surprise from her voice when Freddie nodded. "Can you imagine how difficult it must have been to believe you had a magical whosy-who in your home?" She understood how overwhelming the whole 'magic is real' thing could be, and she wasn't dealing the heartbreak of an injured child.

Freddie turned her, so she was facing him and pressed a kiss to her forehead. His eyes were the color of rich chocolate, and she wondered how dark they turned when he was with a lover. Trying to banish those thoughts before Freddie picked them up, she started to turn back to the painting, but warm hands cupped her shoulders, stilling her.

"Don't ever try to hide your passion, Princess. Your eyes truly are windows into your soul. Your hunger shines brighter than your uncertainty."

Adi felt like a deer caught in the brilliant glare of Freddie's headlights as his gaze held hers. The flare of desire caught as his lips lowered, unhurriedly, to hers. The brush of his heated lips over hers felt like a match touching kindling, the explosion of heat immediate. She leaned close, fisting his shirt in her hands to pull him tight against her. Adi heard the soft moan vibrate up from deep in her chest a heartbeat before the air around her crackled with electricity and a rush of wind encircled them.

"A whosy-who? I'm of the impression that should be a compliment, but I'm not sure I've ever heard that expression before."

Adi jerked her attention to the man sitting casually in one of the wing backed chairs in her sitting room. His long, white beard and flowing purple robe gave him a distinguished air, but it was his sparkling blue eyes that drew her in. He wore small oval, wireless glasses Adi remembered hearing her grandfather refer to as spectacles. One of her few memories of the man was giggling as he searched his office for his *specs*.

"Your grandfather was fun," the man sitting in front of her grinned. "He loved you dearly, Adilei. Rest assured, he is entertaining everyone on the other side of the veil, and he checks on you regularly. He is delighted you've moved home; seems he wasn't a big fan of the sand in Florida."

"Did I say that out loud?" She felt her breath catch as she turned her attention to Freddie.

"No, Princess, but you didn't need to. Your mind is an open book to anyone with the right magic, and I assure you, the Master Wizard sitting in front of you has all the right magical tools."

She turned back to the wizened looking man and blinked in confusion.

"You knew my grandfather? Have we met before? There is something familiar about you. Wait. Christmas Eve. I thought you were Santa." His smile was so bright, she didn't have to wonder if the memory was real. "Your clothes changed right in front of me. I blinked my eyes, and you were dressed in a beautiful red velvet suit. The white fur trim sparkled like it had been sprinkled with diamonds."

"You were such a beautiful child. Full of life and so sure of your place in the world—until your mother passed. I'm thrilled to see that little girl is still inside the lovely young woman you've become." She heard the flirtation in his voice and evidently, Freddie had as well because she could have sworn she heard him cursing under his breath.

"I'm sure the head of the Council on Magic didn't utilize his impeccable timing simply to shower you with compliments about what a lovely child you were, Princess. And I, for one, am interested to hear why he's chosen to pay a social call so late in the evening."

The older man's eyes were twinkling with mischief. He gave Freddie a curt nod, confirming her suspicions the man knew full-well what he'd interrupted. With a casual sweep of his hand, sparkles flew from the tips of his long, slender fingers. The swirl of glittering color encircled them, and Adi felt cocooned… as if he'd made a private room within what was already supposed to be her own space.

"As you have recently learned, the people in the painting can hear what's happening in the room. I want this conversation to be private."

The flirtatious persona was gone, replaced by a man who appeared more like a concerned grandfather than the head of the Council on Magic. For several seconds, Adi's mind raced with questions she wanted to ask, but when she opened her mouth the only thing to spill out was, "What's your name?"

# Chapter Five

S AUL LEANED HIS head back and laughed. He couldn't remember the last time he'd met someone who hadn't instantly known who he was. Despite the two of them having several encounters over the years, she only recalled the first because he'd been surprised to find her standing outside her father's office. Every other time they'd met, he'd been in disguise.

He'd been watching out for her since the day she was born, something he needed to explain sooner rather than later. Understanding their connection would go a long way to convince her selling the house wasn't in anyone's best interest. Well, no one aside from Malcom Bradley, and in Saul's esteemed opinion, the man could burn in hell for what he planned to do to his fellow wizards. He'd known the attorney for more years than he cared to remember, certainly long before he'd been stripped of most of his magical powers. The Kent's had always declined Bradley's less than subtle attempts to buy the house. Emmett had let grief and later, pride stand between him and his only child. As a result, she was completely unaware of the significance of the decision she was facing.

"Before we start discussing business, I want to show

you something. Keep in mind it's been a long time since I needed to prove myself to anyone, so tact might not be my strongest skill." Saul pushed out of his chair and gave her a wicked grin he knew would tell her he was teasing. There wasn't a magical skill he hadn't mastered, a spell he didn't know by heart, a witch or wizard he didn't know personally. *That's what happens when you're two days older than dirt.*

Adilei's violet eyes widened and sparkled with recognition as he morphed into the man she'd seen coming from her father's office many years ago. Before she could begin asking the questions he could feel bubbling to the surface, he changed again. This time he became Santa and handed them both a candy cane.

"I don't understand. Why were you in my father's office? He wasn't a wizard."

Saul and Freddie both chuckled.

"Princess, your father was a very powerful wizard who chose to keep his powers a secret from you. Magic is a Kent family trait." The two of them waited for the full impact of Freddie's words to settle over her. He wasn't surprised to hear her small gasp when she realized what was being implied.

Saul leaned back against the wall with his arms crossed over his chest and watched her for several seconds before pushing back to his full height.

"I could show you lots of other examples of instances when we've met over the years, but to be honest, I'm in a hurry. I've got a date." He almost laughed out loud at the stunned look on Adilei's face. Before she had a chance to embarrass herself asking what was certain to be a very personal question, Saul changed into a popular movie star he knew she would recognize. Her mouthed dropped open, and this time, he couldn't hold back his laughter. *Damn, sometimes it's great to be me.*

FREDDIE LOOKED OVER at Adilei. Her lost expression sent a spear of pain through his chest. Saul had spent over an hour updating her on what they knew about her father's association with Malcom Bradley and what they suspected the attorney was planning. The snake had been plotting for generations to get his magic back and convincing her to sell the house was obviously an important part of his plan.

The mistress of the house was sprawled out on the sofa, staring into the dying flames doing their final flickering dance in the fireplace. She'd muttered something about feeling stupefied by everything she'd learned and shaken her head when he'd tried to talk to her. It would be a lot for anyone to take in. Learning both her parents were *magicals* had thrown her. It had taken everything he had to keep from pulling her into his embrace and assuring her everything was going to be fine, but he'd instinctively known that wasn't what she needed. Adilei wouldn't have appreciated him making her appear weak in front of Saul. He understood the need for dignity when dealing with the Master Wizard. Saul was intimidating even when he wasn't trying to be, and he could be downright terrifying if he made even the smallest effort.

Adilei's soft sigh brought Freddie back to the moment. He leaned forward and slipped his arms around her. "Come here, Princess. I need to hold you." She settled against him, and he could feel the tension draining from her.

"Thank you. I needed this more than I knew."

He didn't like the defeated tone he heard in her voice, but it wasn't a battle he was willing to fight tonight.

"I understand why my mom didn't tell me about the magic. I was incredibly young when she died."

"She was aware of the huge burden she was leaving you. Dealing with the grief of losing your mother was going to be enough, she didn't want to layer another weight on your tiny shoulders." He'd treasured his friendship with Lizette and always regretted she'd been taken from them much too soon. She'd trusted the doctors instead of relying on magic, and it proved to be a fatal error. By the time she petitioned the council for magical help, it was too late.

"My dad should have told me. He had so many opportunities, but he didn't say a word. I just don't understand why. Why would he exclude me from something which was obviously a very large part of who he was?"

He hated hearing the heartbreak in her voice, but it wasn't a pain he could help with... at least not if he was honest with her.

"Your dad made the same mistake many others make; he was convinced he had more time. To be honest, I'm still shocked he's gone." Freddie still wasn't convinced her father hadn't been poisoned, but until he had proof, he wasn't going to worry Adilei unnecessarily. Pulling her onto his lap, he grinned when she squeaked in surprise.

"What are you doing?"

"I've waited years for this moment, Adilei. I want to feel you intimately pressed against me." He also wanted to distract her before she started asking questions he didn't want to answer. If he was right about her father's untimely death, she would also be in danger if she decided to keep the house. His body forced him to push those thoughts aside because he was responding to hers in ways he couldn't have controlled even if he'd wanted to—which he didn't.

Bracketing her face with his hands, Freddie drew the pad of his thumb slowly over her plump lower lip. "I'm going to kiss you, Princess." He didn't give her time to respond before gently brushing his lips over hers. The subtle prelude was like setting a match to kindling. The fire in his soul exploded in a white-hot burst of desire he had no hope of reining in. Pushing his fingers through her hair, Freddie tightened his grip on her and let the intensity of the moment sweep over him. When she moaned into the kiss, he took advantage of the opening and pushed his tongue forward.

Her flavor fused with his own, and between one heart beat and the next, he felt her magic spark to life. The sudden tension in her petite form told him she felt the surge of energy though she might not have registered its meaning. The dominance he'd been forced to suppress for so many years rose quickly to the surface despite his best efforts to control it.

Pulling back, he stared into her eyes. The violet was now so dark, it looked more like the deep purple of a midnight sky. Her breathing was ragged, and he could see her pulse pounding at the base of her slender neck.

"Tell me now if you don't want this, Princess, because we're quickly approaching the point of no return, and once I've had you, you'll belong to me forever."

"Yes. Please. I want you." The halting speech was rife with hunger and was all he needed. Wrapping his arms around her, he quickly recited the spell which would move them from the ground floor to the bed in her suite. Teleporting was disorienting the first few times, so he continued to hold her close until he felt her relax once again.

"Oh, my God. How did you do that?"

"Magic. It has many useful applications. I'll teach them to you. Later. Now, I'm simply going to use it to my advantage." Another quietly murmured spell and they were both naked.

"Holy hell. You really should warn a girl before you strip them, you know." The corners of her kiss swollen lips tipped up, her eyes sparkling with humor.

"No time. I need to be inside you. Now." Rolling her to her back, Freddie's cock slid through her wet folds, but he managed to resist the urge to push himself into her heat. "Mother of God, you are so hot and wet for me. You are deliberately testing my patience, my love. I've been waiting forever for this moment." Pushing himself down, he used his tongue to circle first one areola then the other. A small puff of air over the damp skin drew her nipples up into even tighter peaks. *Beautiful.*

"Please." Her begging was sweet music to his ears, but he wasn't finished tasting her yet.

"I'll give you everything your lovely body is begging for. But not yet." He pushed himself lower to press gentle kisses above her bikini line. "I can smell your body preparing itself for me, Princess." When she tensed beneath him, Freddie shook his head. "Don't. There is no place for embarrassment between lovers, Adilei."

He wasn't surprised she was shy, but it wasn't something he was willing to ignore. "I'm going to enjoy teaching you the joys of pleasure." The Dom, who'd been locked away for so long, came roaring to the surface, and Freddie felt a surge of heat move through him.

"Hold still, Princess. I want to look at this pretty, pink pussy. I'm going to find out if you taste as delectable as you smell." Using the tip of his tongue, Freddie drew a line from the opening of her vagina up to her clit. Circling the tight bud, he was pleased to feel the shudder of her quaking muscles beneath his fingertips. Using his hands, he held the petals of her sex open as he traced the folds and savored the flavor of the woman he planned to claim as his own.

"You taste exquisite, my love, as sweet as a ripe peach and every bit as juicy." She was already gasping for breath, and he'd just started. It gave Freddie a rush to know he could steal her control so quickly. Continuing his sensual assault, he hummed against her sensitive flesh and relished the fresh rush of honey coating his tongue. "I can hardly wait to feel your muscles rippling around me as pleasure overtakes you, milking me of every last drop of my seed."

# Chapter Six

ADI'S ENTIRE WORLD imploded when Freddie's tongue slipped into her, fucking her with its curled length. For several seconds, she swore she was floating over the bed, her back had arched so far off the smooth cotton sheets. In the dark recesses of her mind, she heard him speak to her. He asked her a question she hadn't fully understood, but it didn't matter. She couldn't form a coherent thought if her life depended on it.

She wasn't a virgin, but she was far from experienced. *Who are you kidding? Most of your sexual experience has come from reading.* She'd never had an orgasm during sex and had begun to wonder if she'd ever find a man who could push her over the edge. By the time she finally came back to herself, Adi was certain she would never view the world the same again. Surely the entire planet had tilted on its axis. There was no way everything could possibly be as it had been an hour ago.

"Now, there's an expression every man in the world loves to see." Freddie moved up her body, pressing kisses along his path.

"Blitzed out on sexual ecstasy? Mind blown to bits by a man who is obviously far more experienced than the woman he's just turned into a puddle of goo?" Adi hadn't intended to say the words out loud, but the smile spreading over his face made her glad she had.

"Yes, love, that's the one. The look that tells me I've sent your mind reeling from pleasure. The magic which is made when two souls connect physically, transcends the simplicity of that description because it is so much more than the sum of the parts. Something new is formed when karma is fulfilled," Freddie's voice was pitched low and moved through her subconsciousness like a warm mist over the swamps near her Florida home.

She'd often driven to the swamps to take early morning walks along their edge; watching the fog roll through the trees had fascinated her. Adi imagined the ghosts of past explorers, lost forever in the depths of the Everglades, pushing back into the trees every morning, afraid of discovery in the early morning light. Despite its undeniable beauty, Florida had never felt like home.

"Do you think we managed to create magic, Freddie? Because right now, I'm not sure I have enough functioning brain cells to know up from down." Her body was still tingling in the aftermath of the most powerful pleasure she'd ever known.

FREDDIE UNDERSTOOD FOR the first time the difference between having sex and making love. He would have told anyone who asked that he already knew all he needed to know about the process, but he'd been woefully naïve. Nothing he'd experienced up to this point was remotely close to what he'd just experienced with Adilei. Feeling her body melting against his had been the hottest thing he'd ever experienced. But it was the fusion of their souls which had left him humbled and honored.

Framing her face with his hands, Freddie kissed her softly. The gentle brush of his lips against hers sent a bolt of heat down his spine, and he pulled back before his body wound itself up for round two before she was ready.

"You undo me, love. I'm not sure I have the words to describe how incredible that was. And we created something so much more than simple magic."

"I don't think there's anything simple about magic. Speaking as a person who has only recently learned it really exists, I can assure you it's spectacular; at the same time, it answers a lot of questions I've had over the years."

He heard a thread of amazement in her voice which told him any sexual encounter she'd had before this had been lacking. He was more pleased than he should have been to know he'd given her something no one else had.

"You're right, of course. Magic is not simple, and those of us who have been around it our entire lives shouldn't become so blasé about how truly blessed we are." Freddie took a deep breath and let it out slowly. Even though he'd had centuries to move past the guilt he felt about misusing his gift, there were still times when the memories of his family's disappointment made his heart clench.

"So, there are rules in magic?" Adilei's voice was so full of wonder, it pulled Freddie back from the brink of his despair over what he could never change.

"Princess, everything that has consequences also has rules. The Universe operates on a system of checks and balances. It's what many of the ancients refer to as yin-yang—what Sir Isaac Newton identified as one of the three laws of motion. For every action, there is an equal and opposite reaction is still one of the basics of physics. It's a universal truth and one magicians understand as well as any scientist who's ever lived."

"I'm not sure I understand. Are you saying magicians are scientists?"

"Princess, magicians are scientists of the first order. Remember, science centers around a deep and abiding respect for nature, and no other group of people understands that better than those who are a part of the magical community." Freddie paused, pushing his fingers through the silky strands of Adilei's hair. He'd longed for this intimacy for so long, it was difficult to remember it was finally real and not simply his imagination teasing him once again. "Thank you, Princess."

Adilei lifted herself up onto her elbow and looked at him curiously. He wanted to smile at the way she studied him, but he held still until she worked out whatever was rolling around in that brilliant mind of hers.

"What are you thanking me for, Freddie?"

He leaned forward and pressed his lips against hers; the move wasn't aggressive, but it left little doubt about his intent. She was his now, and he wasn't giving her up.

"Seeing magic through your eyes is a gift. It reminds me I've been given so much, and magic is just one of the gifts I will treasure each and every day."

# Chapter Seven

"THAT MAN IS the reason I can't be trusted with untraceable poison." Adi was vibrating with rage by the time she disconnected the call. "He's surely the most aggravating man on the planet. I've worked with the public for years, and most of my clients were wealthy, entitled, and spoiled rotten, but I swear no one has ever treated me in a more condescending manner." Malcolm Bradly had obviously forgotten Adilei was a grown woman with real-world experience.

A deep chuckle from behind her startled Adi out of her distracted rant. Spinning around, she was surprised to see Saul sitting in a chair she'd never seen before. Shaking her head, Adi flopped into her own seat behind the desk and wondered what it would be like to just pop in on people unannounced.

"It's convenient. I often catch people talking to themselves, so it's informative as well. And as for the chair, I like this one and yours are so... well, ordinary."

"Ordinary? I'm convinced there is nothing ordinary about this house." Adi shrugged when he raised a brow at her grousing. "I'm sorry. I shouldn't take my frustrations out on you, but Malcom Bradley makes my blood boil." Saul's hearty laugh and twinkling eyes pulled her out of her funk, and Adi found herself grinning. "You're spoiling a perfectly good snit, you know." There was nothing in his expression that even vaguely resembled contrition.

Adi hadn't expected Saul to feel any regret about the other man's behavior, but laughing at her frustration was a bit rude, even for a Big Kahuna Magician. Before she could blink, he'd changed into a blonde surfer, complete with board shorts and an obnoxious floral shirt. Adilei burst out laughing at his ridiculous get up. Perhaps it should bother her that he was listening in on her thoughts, but what good would it do?

"Malcom is arrogant and a pompous ass, but that's going to work in your favor, Adi. It would be easy enough for you to simply tell him you have changed your mind about selling the house."

Adi had learned enough over the past few days to know it was impossible to hurry the head of the Wizard Council, so she simply waited. Saul operated on his own timeline, so she gave him time to consider his words.

"The Council and I have been waiting years for the opportunity to settle things with Malcom, once and for all. For the first time, it appears as if we might get the chance."

"If he can no longer do magic, why is he a problem? Well, other than the fact he's a prick?" Adi had given up trying to hide her disdain for the man since it was impossible to conceal her emotions. In the end, it didn't make any difference, and there was a certain freedom in putting it all out there.

Saul grinned at her before raising his hand, making a

circling motion sending sparkles from the end of his fingers, encasing the two of them in a luminescent bubble. "Ordinarily Freddie runs interference for me when I'm here."

"Interference?" Adi wasn't entirely sure what he meant, but she guessed Freddie kept the others in the house from listening in on Saul's private conversations.

"Freddie's been able to block others from eavesdropping for many years. It was one of his first magical skills to be restored, but in this case, he is the one I'm blocking." Adi felt her brows lift in surprise, and when she opened her mouth to protest, he held up his hand. "No need to defend him, what I have to say is not negative. Freddie can now leave the house anytime he wants."

"Are you serious?" Adi gasped and shot to her feet, she was so excited for her friend and lover. "When will you tell him?"

"I won't, you will."

Adi smiled at the way Saul's smile transformed his face from that of a wizened elder to a man who reminded her so much of her grandfather, it was startling. Her memories of him were sketchy because he'd never lived nearby, but she remembered him showing up unannounced a few times when she was a very young child. Before she could mention it to him, Saul continued.

"The Council knows he plans to take you into the painting tonight. Unfortunately, we aren't the only ones who have heard." She could see there was more, but he was choosing his words carefully, so she dug deep for her patience. His mouth formed into a firm line, and he added, "We need for you to keep him in Commonwealth Park."

"Why do we need to stay in the park?" She was confused and suspected Saul was playing her. At the very least, the gleam in his eye told her he wasn't telling her the entire story.

"Trust is so rare in young people now days." Saul shook his head, but his smile told her he wasn't actually scolding her. *He's not leveling with me either.*

SAUL WATCHED HIS great-granddaughter and smiled to himself. It gave him a great deal of satisfaction to see her memories begin to resurface. Her father had done Adilei a great disservice by keeping her isolated from the magical community after her mother's death. Magicians all around the world had mourned her loss, but Emmett Kent III had nearly gone out of his mind when his young wife died. Saul often wondered if Emmett hadn't subconsciously blamed magic for her death. Emmett and Lizette had both believed magic could save her, but she'd asked for help far too late. *Magicians can be as careless with their health as non-magicals and they often forget there are some Universal truths even magic can't transcend.*

The final part of Freddie's debt had been fulfilled when he made love to Adilei. Their joining laid the foundation for a new generation of magicals. The merging of the families had been foretold several centuries earlier, and all the elements of the prophecy pointed to Freddie and Saul's daughter, Catherine being fated mates. Freddie had never believed she was *his fated mate*, and Catherine had agreed. Saul often wondered if Freddie's determination to prove he was right had been partially responsible for his reckless behavior.

Saul also believed Malcom played a part in Freddie's downfall all those years ago, but he needed proof. Malcom and Freddie had been contemporaries and competitors. His knowledge of the laws gave Malcom the advantage when setting up his competition. Putting all the principal players back in the same location on the same night when all the astrological signs were perfectly aligned was tantamount to hitting the wizarding lottery when it came to recreating an event. Freddie was Malcom's one obstacle to Adilei selling the house, and everyone knew it.

It was going to take the combined magic of every member of the Council to keep Adilei safe. They wanted to uncover who'd worked so hard to intercept a prophecy without changing either Freddie's or Adilei's future. It would be dicey, and everyone was going to have to do their part, without Freddie or Adi being aware of the drama playing out around them.

FREDDIE LEANED AGAINST the office door and stared blankly into the wide hall outside the space he'd shared with Emmett for so many years. Hearing Saul tell Adi he could leave the house shocked him though he wasn't sure why. He'd seen the glittering bits of magic floating in the air when he'd made love to Adilei last night, but a part of him had wondered if it hadn't been his own soul spontaneously combusting. He hadn't been a saint by any measure, but he'd never had a sexual experience that compared to what he'd shared with Adilei last night. The intensity of the pleasure had changed everything he thought he knew about sex.

The prophecy about the joining of their magic mentioned the exponential increase they would both experience in their magic, and Freddie had noticed the difference from the moment he'd first awoke this morning. Walking past the Christmas painting, he'd seen elements he'd never noticed before. There were two figures cloaked in the shadows who hadn't been there just a few hours ago. And now, after hearing Saul's conversation with Adilei, he was convinced they were going to be key figures in whatever drama would play out tonight. In the end, knowing why he'd been set up wasn't going to change anything—hell, he didn't *want* to change anything that had happened in the past because every step, as well as each misstep, had led him to Adilei.

Saul's shield of silence wasn't as strong as it had once been, and for the first time, Freddie wondered about the elderly man's health. Wizards might have extended life spans, but none of them would live forever. Freddie wondered how Adilei would feel when she learned Saul was her great-grandfather. Everyone had honored Emmett's wishes to keep Adi from learning about her magical heritage. They'd all known he was making a mistake, but they'd complied out of respect.

Emmett had been terrified Adi would make the same mistake Lizette had made and use magic as a fail-safe. He'd wanted his daughter to make decisions knowing she'd be responsible for their consequences, where his impetuous young wife had always seen magic as her personal get out of jail free card.

The tone of Adilei's voice indicated she was more than a little skeptical, and Freddie grinned. She was questioning Saul's intentions; Adi was smart enough to know he wasn't telling her the whole truth.

With a wave of his hand, Freddie decorated the entire house in the elegant gold and white Christmas decorations he knew Adilei loved. She'd inherited her mother's love for refined décor while he favored the small tree in the servant's quarters. The small tree was always adorned with the ornaments Adilei had made for them over the years. For him, the baubles made of popsicle sticks and yarn held more meaning than the Swarovski and Waterford crystal ornaments, worth thousands of dollars, which had been passed down in her mother's family for generations.

Adilei had asked him to help her decorate after lunch, but now he had other plans. They'd go for the stroll in the painting this evening, just as Saul had requested, but first he wanted to take a carriage ride around Commonwealth park. He'd dreamt of the two of them huddling under a blanket, sipping hot chocolate. Holding her close as they passed under the snow-covered boughs of overhanging trees strung with sparkling lights would be the fulfillment of the first of a long list of *moments* he'd been planning for many years.

All the places he'd thought he wanted to visit *first* faded to the back of his mind. It was supposed to snow again this afternoon, and the sky was already darkening. It would be chilly which meant she'd be snuggled up to him. Having her nestled close as he enjoyed the fresh air for the first time in too many years to count was second only to having her naked flesh pressed against his. Before Freddie could lose himself in that tantalizing fantasy, he felt Saul's magic leave the mansion and heard Adi's soft gasp when she found him leaning against the doorframe of the office door.

Some small part of him had worried she would try to hide her meeting with Saul and all the implications of what she'd heard, but one look at her beaming face banished those fears. Adi grabbed his hand and pulled him into the office.

"Oh my God, Freddie, I have the most amazing thing to tell you." He didn't have the heart to burst her bubble by telling her he'd already heard—her happiness bubbled over as she shared the news.

The absolute joy in her eyes had him blinking back tears of gratitude. Only love could make one person so happy for another. He might not feel as though he deserved her, but that didn't mean he planned to give her up. *Never question why you've been given a gift… let your heart be grateful and the floodgates of the Universe's love will open for you.* The words whispered through his mind, and he smiled when he realized they'd been spoken in Saul's raspy voice.

# Chapter Eight

FREDDIE FELT LIKE a kid allowed to venture out on his own for the first time. With Adilei's dainty hand clasped in his own, they crossed the busy street, and he felt his heart soar as all his favorite landmarks came into view. There were more vendors now, but the layout of the park hadn't changed as much as he'd feared.

Musicians played near the large gazebo, and Freddie pulled Adi into the restored structure to dance. "You feel perfect in my arms, Princess." She didn't miss a step as they waltzed around the beautifully decorated structure.

Adi threw her head back and laughed. "I'm sure people are wondering why we're waltzing to *Rockin' Around the Christmas Tree.*"

"I've learned every new dance craze that's come along, Adilei, but I want to feel the soft pillows of your breasts pressing against me. I want to be able to smell the fresh citrus scent of your hair as it brushes against my cheek. And I want to hear all those sweet sounds you make when you're safely in my arms." Freddie was so enamored with the woman he was waltzing around the beautiful gazebo, he was tempted to cut short his first foray outside and take her back to bed.

"Oh no you don't, I know that look. I want you to

enjoy your freedom for a while longer."

"We'll be back tonight." He was teasing, but he felt her stiffen in his arms. He reluctantly allowed the distance when she pulled back to look into his eyes.

"Will it be the same, Freddie?"

"In some ways it will be hard for you to tell the difference except for the style of clothing." He smiled at the wistful look on her face, but he was worried Adilei would romanticize the experience and become so lost in the moment, she wouldn't be as alert to her surroundings as she needed to be. "Princess, don't be fooled by the beauty you see tonight." She didn't comment, but he could tell by her expression she didn't understand what he meant.

"Think of it this way—the people you'll meet have been stuck in a perpetual state of winter, re-enacting the same roles for many years. Not everyone copes well, and they'll use any opportunity that comes along to lash out at a visitor."

"They'll be angry because we can leave?"

"Envious. Resentful. Angry. The gambit of emotions will be wide, but in the end, it's all basically the same problem. There will be those who will try to prevent our return to the real world. They are my biggest concern."

They would have to join forces because his and Adilei's combined magic was going to be tremendously powerful, but she hadn't learned how to harness the full power of hers yet, so using it would be unpredictable at best. Since he didn't know what Saul was up to, Freddie planned to be even more cautious. Saul had always been crazy about Adilei, and Freddie couldn't imagine the other man putting her in danger, but he wasn't going to take any chances. He was determined to do whatever it took to keep her safe.

Walking around the park, Freddie took note of any area where it would be easy for someone to hide, so he could avoid them tonight when they visited the painting. He helped her into the horse drawn carriage and wrapped them in the soft blanket the driver provided. Leaning close, he whispered against her ear.

"I would like to cancel our plans for this evening; a part of me worries that Saul is endangering you in order to ensnare Malcom." When her eyes widened, he grinned. "Saul's silence shield isn't what it once was."

"Or your magic is getting stronger."

He was impressed she'd drawn that conclusion on her own, but he couldn't say that he was surprised—Adilei had always been incredibly bright.

"Everyone thinks I don't know what's going on, and it's true I'm not as informed as I should be, but I'm intuitive, and you aren't as good at hiding your worry as you think you are."

Freddie framed her face with his hands and pressed his lips against hers. The soft brush was supposed to be a teaser of things to come, but the kiss quickly escalated into a passion-fueled claiming.

"We need to go home, Princess, before I end up having my way with you in this carriage and scandalize both horse and driver."

"Kind Sir, you'd need to have wild monkey sex while hanging over the back of the carriage by your toenails to even get a second look from me." The driver glanced over his shoulder and pulled to a stop right in front of the Kent mansion.

"Wait. How did he know where we were going?" Adilei let Freddie help her from the carriage, but she stood rooted in place when he tried to lead her up the front steps. She could hear the driver's chuckle over the clip clop of the horse's hooves as the carriage moved down the street.

"I know you haven't been home in a long time, Princess, but when was the last time you remember carriage rides around Commonwealth Park?" He watched her eyes widen in surprise, then curiosity, and finally, gratitude.

"I can't believe you created that just for me." She launched herself into his arms, kissing him furiously. When she finally pulled back, he thought this heart would burst from the look of love in her eyes.

"Actually, I just brought them up from Central Park. Orin and Daisy were in the painting until a few years ago. They were thrilled to help; you have always been favored by those in the paintings. Watching you grow up was one of the few gifts we were given, and we treasured it." He watched as she looked down the street, her eyes widening in surprise when she saw the horse and carriage were gone. "They are safely back in New York City. Orin is enjoying his hometown immensely, but he's chosen to keep a relatively low magical profile."

"Will I get to see them again?"

The affection in her voice warmed him from the inside. He'd take great pleasure in sharing carriage rides in Central Park with Adilei.

"Of course. I'm looking forward to exploring the world with you, Princess. When this bit of business is resolved tonight, we'll be free to do as we please." He stared into her eyes; it was so easy to fall into their violet depths. Adilei had no idea how much her magic was growing or how powerful it would eventually become. It was sad the strength of her character had been forged by her father's inattention, and even though those years had been painful for her, they'd also been empowering.

"Does this mean you're staying in Boston? Staying with me?" With his hands framing her face, he could feel the flush before he could see the pink tinge on her cheeks.

"I don't think I have a choice. I couldn't bear to leave you again."

Freddie felt as if the weight of the world had been lifted from his shoulders. He wrapped his arms around Adilei, lifting her feet from the sidewalk, spinning her in a circle. Her tinkling laughter blew the last remnants of sadness from the corners of his soul. He hadn't realized how much of the old guilt still weighed him down until it was gone. Suddenly, the sparkling Christmas lights surrounding them were brighter, the air crisper, and soft strains of the string quartet playing in the gazebo across the street were clearer than they'd been just a moment earlier. Setting her on her feet, he grasped her hand and started up the stairs.

"Come on, love. I've got big plans for you before we go on our little adventure this evening."

"Do those plans include the wild, monkey sex Orin mentioned?"

Freddie nodded and laughed, "I guess we can add telepathy to your growing list of skills, Princess." At her confused look, he chuckled, "Orin didn't speak aloud, and he'd be embarrassed to know you heard his crude remarks."

She gasped in surprise, but didn't miss a step as they sprinted up the stairs to her suite.

ADI'S HEART WAS racing when they burst through the door to her suite of rooms on the third floor, and it wasn't from their mad dash up the stairs. It was the man standing in front of her, his eyes darkening with desire. Freddie's attention was focused entirely on her, and for a moment, Adi was overcome with an emotion she hadn't experienced in so long, she'd almost forgotten what it felt like.

"Naked. Now." His commanding words startled her out of her musings, and Adi didn't hesitate to comply. "Slowly, love. I want to savor this, and it will give you a chance to warm up because I plan to keep you naked for the next several hours."

Her entire body reacted to his words, heating from the inside. *Yeah, warmth isn't an issue now, that's for sure.* As she slipped out of the multiple pieces of clothing she'd donned for their trip to the park, she felt like she was revealing herself to him in *layers*. The word popped into her mind and wasn't easily moved aside.

*Layers. It's all layers, Princess. I promise to explain. Later.*

*But first, I'm going to love you.*

She smiled when she realized it was Freddie who was speaking in her mind. How many times had she erroneously given credit for that inner voice to her subconscious? How often had it been someone who could use their magic to speak to others? Warm hands cupping her shoulders brought her back to the moment, and she was surprised to see Freddie standing right in front of her. *Damn, I really need to pay better attention.*

"Yes, you do. As charming as those little moments of distraction are, they can also be dangerous. When we are alone, I'll relish them because they give me glimpses into the soul of the woman who holds my heart in the palm of her hand. Most men can only dream of being able to understand what their lovers are thinking." He grinned, his eyes dancing with mischief.

Her heart squeezed at the realization she'd loved him her entire life and hadn't known it. He held her chin with his fingers, and she felt his focus narrow.

"Remember, anytime we are outside of this house, you need to be on your guard."

"Outside the house?"

"The entire house is protected, Princess. Ancient spells have held that protection in place for centuries; it's one of the reasons so little has changed inside over the years. Even the smallest renovation takes forever because each step requires a member of the Magical Council to renew and reinforce the original protection spell."

Her head was spinning as she tried to keep up with the deluge of information that seemed to be coming at her in wave after unexpected wave.

"Stay with me, Princess." Freddie's hand slid down over her shoulders to cup her breasts, and she gasped when he gave her nipples a sharp squeeze. "It's time to play, and I want your attention focused entirely on the pleasure I'm giving you."

A second pinch made her moan, earning a smile from the man standing so close, she could feel the heat of his body wrapping around her. Leaning down, he circled her areola with the tip of his tongue, soothing the smarting flesh. "Are you wet for me, love?" The words were pitched low and dripped with sensuality, setting a firestorm of heat in her core.

"Yes. Always." Adi barely recognized her own voice, it was so filled with desire. When Freddie's fingers slid through her slick folds, her legs parted of their own volition. She worried her knees were going to buckle out from under her, they were shaking so badly. Before she could blink, the two of them were lying on the bed, and Freddie's tongue was retracing the same path his fingers had taken a few seconds earlier. Digging her heels into the bed, Adi arched against the sweetest torture she'd ever known.

"Stay still, or I'll tie you to the bed, Princess." Before the words had even registered, her body reacted, sending a rush of cream to coat his tongue. "You like the idea of being bound, don't you, love? You are so fucking perfect. Someday soon, we'll go to Japan and watch a Shibari demonstration. It's pure erotic art, and no one does it better."

Adi wanted to respond, but he sucked hard on her clit, scraping the sensitive bundle of nerves against his teeth. The move turned her mind to mush, and fireworks began bursting behind her eyelids, the heat radiating from the very center of her being to sear every cell in her body. She heard herself scream Freddie's name, and somewhere in the back of her mind, she felt him move over her.

The burn of swollen tissues stretching when he pushed his cock deep was exactly what Adi needed to catapult her over the edge of oblivion once again. When she tried to wrap her arms around him, she realized they were tethered over her head, and her pussy contracted in response.

"Fucking perfect. You amaze me. You own me. You. Are. *Mine!*" Freddie timed his thrusts with his words, then practically roared the last one as she felt hot pulses of his release splash against her cervix. The room spiraled around her as another orgasm branded his name on her soul. Adi struggled to stay focused on the man looking down at her as if she'd personally hung the moon and stars, but sweet oblivion was pulling her quickly away from reality.

Adi was floating in a mind fog and wanted desperately to close her eyes and drift off to sleep. Damn, Freddie had fried her brain. She felt him shift, then a warm cloth cleaning between her thighs. *So sweet. I'm so spoiled. Just a little nap and I'll make dinner.* Soon, she was cocooned in warmth as strong arms pulled her against a masculine chest. The thumping of Freddie's heart lulled her to sleep as he sang what sounded like an ancient Celtic tune and pressed kisses against her hair.

# Chapter Nine

FREDDIE HELD ADILEI'S hand as they stood shoulder to shoulder, gazing into the painting. They'd taken a short nap, made love again, then destroyed the fruit and cheese platter the cooks had left outside the door. He could have easily done it himself with little more than a nod of his head, but he appreciated their thoughtfulness. That's the way it had been inside the Kent mansion for over two centuries, and he hoped it was a tradition Adilei would want to continue. Helping those in the magic community who deserved a second chance was worth the chance they were about to take by entering the painting.

"Can my mom visit me in a painting?"

Her softly spoken question tugged at his heart. He hated to be the one to tell her; this was probably going to one of many difficult lessons she'd need to learn about the magical world.

"Not in the way you're asking, love. Wizards are like everyone else when it comes to death. We move to the other side of the veil and continue our work."

"Work?"

He doubted she was as confused as she sounded; he knew her well enough to recognize when he'd piqued her curiosity.

"Yes, our souls come here to make whatever changes we can, then we return to the other side, but we continue to help by infusing what we've learned into the minds of those still on this plane." This time, her confused look was sincere, and he shook his head. "You're thinking of it as a curtain drawn between two sides of existence, and that's over-simplifying it." Pursing his lips, Freddie searched for the right words—words which would help her understand how close her mother was each and every day.

Stepping behind her, Freddie slid his hands under her sweater and traced a line along the waistband of her jeans. He let his fingers trace slow circles over her bare stomach and wondered how soon he would see her round with his child. He'd waited so long, but they needed to spend time enjoying one another before they added the challenges a child would bring. Their children would be magical royalty, treasures from the joining of two titan magical families, fulfilling a prophesy as old as the earliest oral histories passed down one generation to the next. Refocusing his attention on their discussion, Freddie leaned forward and kissed the sensitive place below her ear.

"Have you ever seen the way animators create movies?" When she nodded, he could see the question in her eyes, so he continued, "Layers of drawings are put together until they form what we see when we watch their creation. Existence is essentially the same. There are layers upon layers, but most people only see a few of the layers rather than the finished product. They have no idea there are many different parts of the whole. The background is a layer, and the people you can see are another, but there are also portions which are not always visible to the human eye. The other side is just another layer of existence layered over the top of what you see. And magic is simply a way of moving things between the layers."

She watched him for several long seconds, and he could almost hear her mind spinning as she mulled over what he'd said. "You're telling me my mom is always nearby, aren't you? That she's as close as a whispered prayer, near enough to touch if I'll just open my heart to things my eyes can't see."

Goddess he loved this woman. She not only understood what he'd said, she'd taken it to a level he hadn't wanted to approach, yet, in fear he'd frighten her. In his experience, people who aren't exposed to magic as children often didn't ever develop imaginations capable of fully understanding how remarkable the Universe is.

"Your ability to grasp abstract concepts amazes me, Princess. I can feel your magic gaining strength every day."

"It might be getting stronger, but I don't have any idea how to use it."

The insecurity in her voice had him shaking his head. No woman should ever be made to feel like they aren't good enough. In his opinion, any man who belittled his woman was a sick bastard who didn't deserve the feminine gift he'd been given. Freddie had seen it many times over the years, and the cruelty of emotional abuse always made his anger boil over.

"Magic is like everything else—it's a learned skill, but there are also people like you who have an abundance of natural talent. Some of it will come to you when you need it most. The most important thing for you to remember is follow your heart. If you listen to situations with your heart, you'll never go wrong."

She nodded, and he stepped back to grab their winter wear. It wouldn't be as cold in the painting as it had been this afternoon in the park and certainly not as cold as it would be outside tonight. Freddie had already stashed a number of magical protection stones in her coat pockets, along with a small satchel full of an herb mixture one of the local witches had put together for tonight's adventure. It was obvious Freddie hadn't been the only one eavesdropping on Adilei and Saul's conversation earlier today because most of the house wizards were gathering in nearby paintings. They would step into the suite as soon as he and Adi entered the painting. Their combined magic would be a tremendous help when they were ready to return.

He didn't give her a chance to overthink the situation; as soon they'd donned their coats, hat, and gloves, he muttered a short protection spell, then pushed them through the veil into the painting. She swayed, but her booted feet remained firmly planted, and he smiled at the deer in the headlights glaze in her eyes.

"It's disorienting until you get used to it. It's more difficult than simply traveling from one place to another on the same plane." Adilei nodded, but he wasn't sure she'd fully understood what he'd said. Freddie watched as she looked around them, a huge smile pushing aside the confusion.

"It's remarkable. I feel like I've been transported back in time; what an amazing privilege, to be able to experience this."

They walked hand in hand, exploring the park, but he was careful to steer her away from the places he'd identified as potentially dangerous. They rode the carousel, and watching the enchanted look on her face as the lights twinkled around her, made his heart swell with love.

"Where did you live, Freddie?" Adilei's question surprised him, but it probably shouldn't have. She'd always been inquisitive.

"My family home was just across the street from yours." They were sitting outside the gazebo listening to Christmas music, and he wondered what had prompted her to ask. She turned slightly to face him and gave him a sad smile.

"Did you ever see anyone in your family again after being locked in the painting?"

"No one close, no. My parents moved and sold the house. I brought them nothing but shame, Princess. Over the years, I was able to restore the family name and rebuild the fortune I'd squandered; I only wish they'd lived to see me redeem myself." It was one of the few regrets he hadn't been able to let go.

His father had been a harsh man with unreasonable expectations which had been impossible to meet, but that didn't mean Freddie hadn't wished a thousand times the man had lived long enough to witness his comeback. When she didn't respond, he gave her a small smile and realized he hadn't thought about his family home in a long time.

"The house was eventually razed in the name of progress, and from what I heard, it had fallen into a sorry state of disrepair. This afternoon was the first time I'd seen the improvements made to what you call the Historic District." He kissed the tip of her nose and the frown lines between her drawn brows before pressing his warm cheek against her cool one.

"We're going to have a nice, long, naked chat about that expression, Princess. Frowning at a sexual dominant is never wise." He could feel the electricity humming through her body, the sweet anticipation of what he'd just promised.

"I'll look forward…" This time the surge of power pulsing around them was much different—this was born of uncertainty, bordering on fear. When he would have pulled back, she grasped the lapels of his jacket and held him close.

"Wait, I don't want to tip off the couple walking toward us. There's something familiar about the woman, but her face is shadowed by her cloak. The man looks a lot like Malcom, but he's much younger."

"Malcom would appear much younger. Entering the painting means he'll appear as he did when it was created. He's lost so much of his magic, his body now ages at a faster rate than most magicals." He'd already explained once wizards reach adulthood, their aging slows, but this was the first time he'd told her there were exceptions, and Malcom Bradley was one of the best 'bad' examples around.

"They are both far too interested in what we're doing, but I don't think their interest is the same. His focus is malevolent, but hers isn't. She seems more... I don't know how to describe it, enthralled is the only word that comes to mind. I get the idea she's admiring us. She wants to make contact."

Adilei's words were like the lash of a whip, and in the blink of an eye, Freddie knew how Malcom planned to *persuade* her to sign over the house. If she signed it over now, the future of magic would be changed from this time forward. Freddie wrapped his arms tightly around her just as she attempted to pull out of his arms.

"It's her. It's my mother."

# Chapter Ten

ADILEI FELT THE turbulence of Freddie's emotions at the same moment his arms tightened around her. Looking into eyes which looked so much like her own, Adi's entire body felt as if she'd been hit by lightning.

"It's her. It's my mother." Before she'd even uttered the words, Freddie's arms had tightened anchoring her to his chest. "Let me go, Freddie. I want to see my mom."

"Stop. Think, Adilei. Why would your mother be here? Why would she be on the arm of a man she hated?" Freddie's word barely penetrated the haze of emotion surrounding her.

"Hated? I thought they were friends?" She was talking to him, but her eyes hadn't left the couple moving slowing in their direction.

"They were, for many years, but Malcom slowly slid toward the dark arts which began to cause a lot of friction between the three of them. When she got sick, she asked Malcom to help her find a doctor. She foolishly listened to his advice and discovered too late, he'd deliberately led her astray."

Adi felt like she was going to explode with rage. The man who'd pretended to be her father's closest friend had been the one responsible for their years of grief. It seemed so unfair; she couldn't wrap her mind around all the possible implications.

"The woman with him is an imposter?" Her heart felt like it was being torn in two. A part of her wanted to run into her mother's arms, but the rational part knew this was the cruelest trick anyone had ever played on her. Baiting a trap using a child's love for a lost parent was beneath vile.

"Yes, Princess, and Malcom's magic isn't strong enough to pull this off alone, so we need to find out who's helping him."

Saul had told her there were other forces at work the night Freddie was sent into the painting, but she hadn't expected the burning sense of betrayal now festering in her heart.

Adi hid her eyes from the couple as they drew closer, hoping they hadn't realized they'd caught her interest. Burying her face against Freddie's neck, she pretended to close her eyes, but kept them open enough to see the frustrated look on Malcolm's face. He spoke to the woman, and she immediately pushed the hood of her cloak back, leaving no doubt who she was impersonating.

*Let Saul and the others do their jobs, Princess.* Freddie's soothing words settled in her mind, and she pulled in a deep breath. The familiar scent of his skin calmed her further, and this time, she fully closed her eyes, blocking out the couple now close enough she could hear their voices.

"She is too busy acting like a floosy to pay attention

to her own mother, can you imagine?"

Any doubt Adi had about the woman on Malcom's arm evaporated into a fine mist under the heat of her anger. Her mother had never spoken ill of anyone and certainly, wouldn't have done so to her own daughter. She felt Malcom's glare, and all the emotions she'd held inside since her mother was stolen from her roared to the surface.

Adi stepped around him before Freddie could stop her. A vision of her mother, dressed in a midnight blue cloak decorated with shimmering stars shooting across the surface, flashed in her mind, and she heard her mother's sweet voice whisper to her soul.

*You have all the tools you need, Princess. Everything you need to defend the one you love is within your reach... you need only ask.*

She sucked in a breath and swayed on her feet as electricity crackled around her, sparks lighting the air in small bursts, so brilliant they hurt her eyes. Freddie's arms wrapped around her, but not before she'd raised her hand, pointing a finger at the duo who appeared more than ready for the coming confrontation.

"Be gone, imposter. You can duplicate someone's appearance, but the facade doesn't hide a black heart. Costumes don't fool love." Adi's entire body was burning, and inside she was shaking like a leaf, but much to her relief, her hand was steady as a rock.

*Don't let them bait you, Princess. They both know they'll lose.*

Freddie's words pulled her back from the razor-sharp edge of rage she'd been skating on, and she sucked in a deep breath. Adi looked from the man to the woman, then back at Malcom, and raised a brow.

"What made you think this would work? And what did you hope to gain? Did you think it would be funny to fool me into thinking your floosy friend is my mother?"

She watched his reactions closely, and he seemed surprisingly unaffected at the insult to his accomplice. His complete lack of chivalry seemed odd given the circumstances; it was supposed to be a time when opening doors for a woman was considered an act of respect rather than an insult. Her friends often told her she'd been born a century or two later than her soul; they were probably right. She had never understood how common courtesy could be construed as insulting.

The woman stared at her as if she'd suddenly sprouted horns before huffing a string of curses that would make a sailor blush. She ended her tirade and leaned forward in an unsuccessful attempt to intimidate Adi.

"Be gone? Who do you think you are? Your lover may call you Princess, but men will say anything if it will get them between your thighs. You are going to learn just how insignificant you are, Miss Kent."

The woman was practically hissing, and Adi thought the snake comparison was probably more accurate than she knew.

When the woman started to raise her hand, Malcom wrapped his hand around her wrist holding her still and fixing his gaze on Adi. "There is no need to be rude, Adilei. That isn't the way your parents raised you. Clearly Freddie is a poor influence, something I'm sure the council is watching closely."

*He thinks I'm rude? Really? Did he even hear that bitch standing next to him? I'll show him rude.* For just a moment, Adi wondered if her behavior was putting Freddie's freedom in jeopardy, but then she heard him chuckle softly beside her.

"You continue to surprise me, Malcom. Every time I think your ethics have reached their lowest, you move the bar down a peg or two. You've used the image of Adilei's mother, and now, you're attempting to use her lover in a lame attempt at guilt. You really are losing your touch."

For the first time, Adi saw a chink in the man's armor. Malcom was well and truly pissed, and it showed. There was a back haze surrounding him, and it took her a few seconds to realize she was seeing his aura. The darkness in this man went all the way to the depths of his soul; no wonder the council wanted to take him down once and for all.

"Your father wanted you to sell the house, Adilei—you know this. He had no use for magic after your mother's death. It let him down, and he wanted nothing to do with it." His voice had taken on a strange tone which would have been convincing if she hadn't already known his motives were anything but altruistic.

"Magic didn't let him down, you did. Your phony friendship was the ultimate betrayal. Pretending to be someone's friend, letting them believe you care about their happiness and their well-being when you're trying to wrest control of their home out from under them is beyond contemptuous. You are abhorrent to everything magic stands for." She wasn't sure where all the venomous words had come from, but the warmth of her mother's love radiated from her heart, moving through her entire body as if charging every cell with energy.

SAUL WATCHED FROM his position a few feet from where Adilei Kent stood facing off with Malcom Bradley. The attorney was seething, and it was only a matter of time before he showed his hand. Freddie had been right when he'd told Adi that Saul's power wasn't what it had once been, but what the younger man didn't know was the entire magic community had been fading. The prophecies of old foretold of a princess rising from the ashes of a royal family decimated by the dark side of power. The princess would restore the magic of everyone practicing on the side of light and love.

Those who didn't understand the language of the ancients had often looked to those the world considered royalty, but that was inconsistent with the language of the time. Royal families in the ancient magic world were those who'd stood against the forces of evil from the beginning. Their royal status was a matter of honor rather than lineage. White magic's princess was destined to infuse them all with a renewed sense of purpose and power.

Authority was radiating around Adilei, the air around her practically pulsing from the energy, but Malcom seem oblivious to the charged ions emitting small bits of light. His companion's disguise was literally dissolving from the positively charged air. *Light is the only thing that can dispel darkness.* He wanted to smile at the line from the prophesy—rarely had they seen the words play out so graphically.

"You will sell the house as your father requested or face the consequences, Adilei. I've gone out on a limb to protect your reputation, and it's time to pay the piper. You have no idea the wrath you're facing. The debt is huge, and I'm not willing to take the blame for your lack of respect for those who have waited patiently for this day to arrive. Your mother paid for her lack of faith with her life—will you make the same mistake?"

Saul shook his head; Malcom's desperation was almost palatable.

"I'll sell when and if I'm ever inclined to do so. I won't be forced by you or anyone else claiming I owe them some debt I never incurred."

Adilei's voice was laced with confidence and an inner resolve Saul remembered hearing in her mother's voice. Casting a quick spell for Adi's protection, Saul moved deeper in the shadows; he didn't want to risk drawing Malcom's attention.

The rogue wizard had been stripped of most of his powers, but he would recognize the energy storm swirling around Adilei and wonder why some of that energy was being funneled to the man standing off to the side. The strength Saul was gaining was nothing compared to what the Universe was bestowing on Adilei. It had been centuries since he'd seen such a huge outpouring of energy.

Two other women stepped forward to flank Malcom

and his companion. Saul watched their features morph into the men he and his fellow council members suspected were involved with the plot to take over the Kent Mansion, but they hadn't seen any concrete proof, until now.

No one outside of the Council of Magic fully understood the significance of the structure. One of the council's biggest concerns was Malcom's push to gain control of the property. Saul suspected the man was piecing the truth together, and that was a disaster in the making. The council had managed to keep the depth and strength of the crystal line beneath the house a secret for three centuries, and he didn't intend for the information to become public now.

*Good intentions without action are just empty promises.*

# Chapter Eleven

F REDDIE WOULDN'T HAVE recognized the council members, but their magic was so powerful, it threatened to bowl him over. Wizards learned to recognize the magical signatures of their peers, but it took years before most could detect the subtle differences in those at the top echelons of magic. Freddie could feel the distinctive magic of each of the council members—they were here in force.

After centering himself, Freddie was able to pinpoint the location of each member of the council. The fact they were short one member wasn't lost on him. Josiah's death hadn't been a surprise, but his death had cast a shadow over the entire magical community. Freddie could only imagine the political posturing which must be taking place by those anxious to fill the ancient wizard's position. In Freddie's opinion, it was going to take someone with an extraordinary understanding of recovery to replace the name wizards, the world over, considered the champion of the healed souls.

Watching Adilei face-off with Malcom filled Freddie with pride. She might underestimate her magical power, but the truth was soon going to be undeniable. He could feel the storm brewing in her, and Malcom was about to feel the full force of her years of suppressed fury. His soul mate was about to teach the greedy bastard a valuable lesson—a lesson Freddie doubted the other man was going to survive.

Freddie had already cast the strongest protection spell in his arsenal around her, but he felt the magic of the council members' spells layer over top of his incantation a heartbeat before Adilei waved her hand in a gesture of dismissal Malcom wouldn't miss. In this instance, Freddie's years of experience put him ahead of the game, and what he saw play out in his mind's eye was terrifying.

Hearing people describe events as playing out in slow motion is nothing like experiencing it, and Freddie's mind was racing despite the freeze frames clicking one at a time around him. Adilei made a beginning wizard's mistake when she began turning away from her enemy, but she saw Malcom move in her peripheral vision. Freddie wasn't surprised to see light stream from her fingertips as a protective shield, but was shocked to his toes to see her protect him rather than herself.

*Why are you surprised, Freddie? Love is the most powerful magic of all.*

Lizette Kent's sweet voice whispered in his mind as he watched Adilei collapse beside him. A fraction of a second later, Malcom and his companions disintegrated into a fine mist. The power coming from multiple locations, including his own, had been enough to gain the attention of everyone in the painting. Chaos erupted around him, but Freddie's entire world narrowed to the woman laying limp at his feet.

ADILEI HOPED SOMEONE got the tag number of the truck that hit her. Fighting to pull air into her lungs was excruciating, but it was the waves of sorrow washing over her that threatened to pull her under. The man holding her in his arms was inconsolable, and she knew if she didn't pull in a breath soon, he was going to have a reason to be upset. She was teetering on the edge of consciousness.

Through the myriad of voices surrounding her, Adi heard her mother's tinkling laughter float through her mind before her words registered. *He loves you with everything he is, Princess, just as your father and I did. Hold tightly to that gift and let love light your way.* Adi basked in the warmth of her mother's love and relaxed as air filled her lungs. Hearing that her father had loved her filled her heart with a peace she wasn't sure she'd have found on her own.

"Yes, Princess. Breathe for me, love. Come on." Freddie's lips sealed over hers and warm air filled her lungs again. Two breaths filled with love... one from her mother, the other from the man who held her heart. When her eyes opened, Freddie's concerned face was all she could see. He was silhouetted by the twinkling Christmas lights and softly falling snow. She could hear the murmur of voices blending with the music playing nearby, but nothing mattered aside from the love she saw in Freddie's eyes.

The only time he frowned was when she struggled

back to her feet, but she wasn't going to lie around looking pathetic. And she damn sure wasn't going to let Malcom know he'd hurt her. When Freddie chuckled, she looked at him.

"What's so funny?"

"You, Princess. There is no need to worry about Malcom, he and his cohorts were blown to bits." She stared at him, completely shocked by the casual way he'd just described the deaths of three people. He shrugged, "If you're waiting for me to apologize for defending you, you'll be waiting until the end of time, Princess. And for the record, my magic was added to that of the other council members, and it seems the sum of our magic was more powerful than any of us imagined."

"So, the threat to me is gone, now?"

Saul stepped up beside her, his face brighter than it had been during their earlier conversation. *Perhaps he was more concerned than I realized or maybe vaporizing the bad guys was invigorating?*

"Adilei, you are an absolute delight, and I'm thrilled that you are Freddie are mated."

*Mated?*

"Oh yes, indeed. There are various ways to solidify a magical union. The joining of souls through intimacy and acts of love are two of the most binding." He leaned forward and kissed her on each cheek. "You've made your great-grandfather very proud, Princess. Now it's time for the two of you to enjoy your honeymoon before your mate begins his internship with the council."

"Internship? Sir?" Freddie's astonished voice sounded

from beside her.

"Great-grandfather? Honeymoon?"

Adi and Freddie had spoken at the same time, and Saul leaned his head back and laughed. "Off with you. Enjoy your stay on the island, everything there is for your enjoyment. I'll see to it the house is taken care of; your things are already at your destination."

Adi opened her mouth to protest, but before she could utter a sound, she found herself standing in the shade of a giant palm tree, Freddie holding her hand. She looked down at her clothing and laughed; she was wearing a string bikini and her bare toes were buried in the warm sand.

"I'd say your great-grandfather is anxious to become a great-great-grandfather," Freddie nodded to her skimpy attire and his own low-slung swim trunks.

"I have a million questions for him. I suspect you have some of your own." Adi couldn't help but giggle when Freddie pulled her against his warm chest.

"I do indeed, and I'm sure he'll answer them all in good time. But for now, I'm very content to enjoy our time together. I've never celebrated the holidays in the Caribbean, and I'm looking forward to seeing how Christmas lights look in palm trees." Adi couldn't have agreed more. Stretching up on her tip-toes, she lost herself in his kiss. All her questions could wait.

## THE END

# Books by Avery Gale

## The ShadowDance Club
Katarina's Return – Book One
Jenna's Submission – Book Two
Rissa's Recovery – Book Three
Trace & Tori – Book Four
Reborn as Bree – Book Five
Red Clouds Dancing – Book Six
Perfect Picture – Book Seven

## Club Isola
Capturing Callie – Book One
Healing Holly – Book Two
Claiming Abby – Book Three

## Masters of the Prairie Winds Club
Out of the Storm
Saving Grace
Jen's Journey
Bound Treasure
Punishing for Pleasure
Accidental Trifecta
Missionary Position
Another Second Chance

## The Wolf Pack Series
Mated – Book One
Fated Magic – Book Two
Tempted by Darkness – Book Three

**The Knights of the Boardroom**
Book One
Book Two
Book Three

**The Morgan Brothers of Montana**
Coral Hearts – Book One
Dancing with Deception – Book Two
Caged Songbird – Book Three
Game On – Book Four
Well Bred – Book Five

**Mountain Mastery**
Well Written
Savannah's Sentinel
Sheltering Reagan

**The Christmas Painting**

I would love to hear from you!

Website:
www.averygalebooks.com/index.html

Facebook:
facebook.com/avery.gale.3

Twitter:
@avery_gale